DREAMWORKS

DRAGONS

How to Start a DRAGON ACADEMY

adapted by Erica David

HODDER CHILDREN'S BOOKS

First published by Simon Spotlight
An imprint of Simon & Schuster Children's Publishing Division
1230 Avenue of the Americas, New York, New York 10020

First published in Great Britain in 2017 by Hodder and Stoughton

A CIP catalogue record for this book
is available from the British Library.

ISBN 978 1 444 93433 5

Printed and bound in China by RR Donnelley Asia Printing Solutions Limited

The paper and board used in this book are made from wood from responsible sources

Hodder Children's Books
An imprint of
Hachette Children's Group
Part of Hodder and Stoughton
Carmelite House
50 Victoria Embankment
London EC4Y 0DZ

An Hachette UK Company
www.hachette.co.uk

www.hachettechildrens.co.uk

Vikings and dragons used to be enemies.
Then Hiccup met his dragon, Toothless,
and they became best friends.

Now Vikings and dragons lived side by side on Berk.

Most Vikings were happy to share their home with dragons. But sometimes the dragons got into trouble.

The dragons scared fish out of the
Vikings' nets. They chased sheep out
of their pens. And they stole food.

Usually the Vikings could forgive the dragons. But some Vikings got angry when the dragons ate their food. They were trying to store food for the winter freeze.

There was one Viking named Mildew who was very upset. The dragons ate his entire field of cabbage!

"Stoick, you need to put those dragons in cages!" Mildew shouted. "If you don't, they will eat us out of house and home!"

"They don't mean any harm," Hiccup replied. "They are just dragons being dragons."

Chief Stoick told Mildew he would handle the dragons.

That night Hiccup asked Stoick if he could help with the dragons.

"You?" Stoick asked.

"If anyone can control them, I can," Hiccup said.

Stoick decided to give Hiccup a chance.

The next day Hiccup and Toothless went to the village square. Hiccup felt confident that he could get the dragons under control.

The dragons were up to their usual
tricks. Hiccup watched as a Deadly
Nadder sneaked up to a house to
steal a loaf of bread.

Hiccup chased after the Nadder
and placed a hand on his nose. "No!"
Hiccup said firmly.

The Deadly Nadder listened and dropped
the bread.

But while Hiccup was training one dragon, other dragons made trouble all over the village.

Hiccup tried to stop them but it was no use. It began to look like he was helping the dragons break things!

Hiccup realised he couldn't train the dragons alone.

The next day Hiccup invited his friends and their dragons to the arena.

"The dragons are out of control," he said. "We want them to live in our world without destroying it, but they can't without our help."

Hiccup showed his friends how to scratch under a dragon's chin to get it to drop stolen food.

It seemed like they were making progress. But when they headed into the village to find dragons to train, there were no dragons in sight.

Suddenly they heard a loud crash!
Hiccup and his friends rushed towards
the noise. When they arrived, they were
shocked.

The dragons had broken into the village storehouse and eaten all the food that the Vikings were storing for the freeze!

Even Toothless was guilty.

Soon Mildew and the other Vikings arrived. They were very angry.

"You need to send these dragons away!" Mildew shouted.

"You're right, Mildew," Chief Stoick said.
"We will cage them tonight, and Hiccup
will send them away in the morning."

At dinner Hiccup and his friends were very sad. They didn't want to send their dragons away. But Hiccup had an idea.

"The dragons are going to do what they're going to do," Hiccup told his friends. "It's in their nature. We just have to learn to use it."

The next day Hiccup and his friends decided to work with the dragons – not against them.

The dragons scared fish into the
Vikings' nets and chased sheep into
their pens.

The dragons planted food instead of
stealing it. They even helped Mildew
plant his field!

"Great job, dragons!" the Vikings cheered.

Chief Stoick was so proud of Hiccup and his friends, he gave them their very own dragon training academy.

Hiccup was excited. He couldn't wait to begin.

"Dragons are powerful, amazing creatures," he said. "And I'm going to learn everything about them."